To remember what you've read, write your initials in a square!

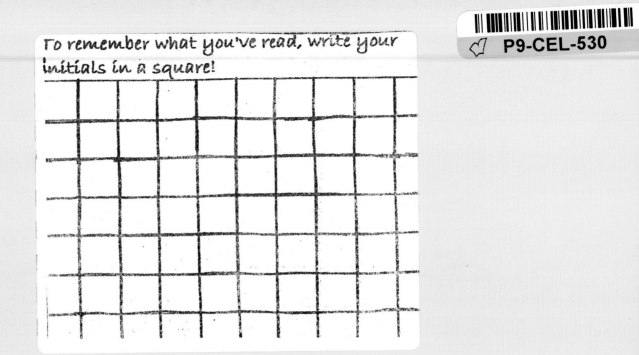

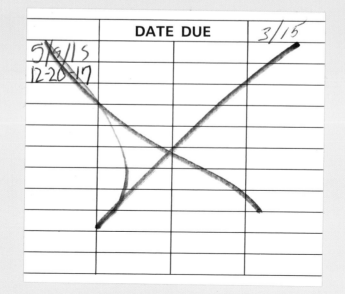

YOU NEST HERE WITH ME

Jane Yolen and Heidi E.Y. Stemple

Illustrations by Melissa Sweet

BOYDS MILLS PRESS
AN IMPRINT OF HIGHLIGHTS
Honesdale, Pennsylvania

My little nestling, time for bed.
Climb inside, you sleepyhead.

Like baby bird, your nest can be
Anywhere there's you and me.

Pigeons nest on concrete ledges,

Catbirds nest in greening hedges,

Tiny wrens, in shoreline sedges.
You nest here with me.

Grackles nest in high fir trees,

Terns all nest in colonies
Upon high cliffs, above rough seas,

But you nest here with me.

Some owls nest in oak tree boles,
Some down in abandoned holes,

Hawks may nest on telephone poles,

But you nest here with me.

Coots nest low in cattail reeds,
Sparrows' nests are full of weeds,
Plus tangled grasses, feathers, seeds . . .

But you nest here with me.

Swallows nest above barn doors,

Plovers nest on sandy shores,

Eagles nest upon high tors,

But you nest here with me.

Cowbird, the uninvited guest,
Leaves her egg in a foster nest—

But you nest here with me.

Killdeer, once their eggs are laid,
Perform a broken-wing charade.

The clutch can rest there unafraid,
As you nest here with me.

Birds nest in trees, in sand, on stone,
In colonies or all alone.
They nest in holes and under eaves,
In barns, in reeds, on poles, in leaves.
And safe inside, the nestlings grow
While learning all they need to know.

So till you're big as big can be . . .
You'll nest right here
in our house
with me.

AUTHORS' NOTE

Everyone in our family is a bird watcher. David Stemple (Jane's husband and Heidi's dad) was a very serious bird watcher, traveling all over the world to spot rare birds to add to his life list. Heidi, an owl enthusiast, gets up very late at night to call up owls as part of the National Audubon Christmas Bird Count each year. Her record is 67 owls in one night. Jane prefers to watch and listen in her own backyard, which she keeps wild and green and filled with trees where birds of all kinds make their nests. But no matter where you live— in the desert, on the coast, in the mountains, or in a city—you can spot birds. Even in the pages of this book, you may find a few surprises. Can you spot the nuthatch, cardinal, robin, and hummingbird?

PIGEON

- Also called Rock Doves, pigeons were introduced to the Americas in the 1600s.
- They eat just about anything, although their natural diet is mostly grains and seeds.
- During World Wars I and II, the U.S. Army sent messages using pigeons.
- Females sit patiently while their mates bring nest-building materials one twig at a time.

CATBIRD

- Catbirds can be spotted almost everywhere in the U.S. except the Pacific coast.
- They eat mostly insects but also fruits when available.
- Named for their call, catbirds sound just like a mewing cat.
- Catbirds make open, cup-shaped nests with finely woven linings.

WREN

- Different types of wrens can be found all over the Americas.
- They eat whichever small critters are in season—insects, spiders, snails, and others.
- Most wrens can be identified by their up-tipped tail.
- Marsh and Sedge Wrens make round nests in shoreline grasses and sedges.

COOT

- Coots are found all over the U.S. and Mexico as well as parts of Canada.
- Though mainly plant-eaters, coots will also eat small creatures.
- To fly, coots run clumsily across the water, flapping their wings.
- Coot nests are woven, floating creations anchored to stalks of vegetation.

SPARROW

- Thirty-five types of sparrows live in North America, but sparrows can be found almost everywhere in the world.
- These small birds eat seeds, grain, insects, and other creatures.
- The most common sparrow in the U.S. was originally from Europe.
- The House Sparrow is messy, overstuffing its nest with grass and other materials.

SWALLOW

- Some North American swallows are named for habitats: Barn, Cliff, and Cave Swallows.
- They eat mostly flying insects.
- Some young swallows help out their parents by returning to the nest to feed their siblings.
- The Barn Swallow usually makes mud-and-straw nests on man-made structures.

GRACKLE

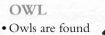

- The U.S. and Mexico are home to Common, Boat-Tailed, and Great-Tailed Grackles.
- Their diet includes seeds and small creatures such as beetles, fish, and mice.
- Grackles let ants climb on them— perhaps, according to scientists, to kill parasites.
- Female grackles sometimes change their minds about nest sites even while the male builds.

TERN

- Terns are water birds that live near the ocean.
- Their diet consists almost entirely of fish.
- Terns drink saltwater by dipping their beaks into the ocean while flying.
- Terns nest in big groups called colonies, usually with little or no nesting material.

OWL

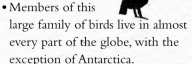

- Owls are found everywhere on earth except Antarctica.
- Most owls are nocturnal birds of prey who hunt for mice, bugs, and birds at night.
- Owls' feathers are built for flying soundlessly.
- Most owls are "opportunistic nesters," using existing nests or holes to lay their eggs.

HAWK

- Members of this large family of birds live in almost every part of the globe, with the exception of Antarctica.
- Their diet includes all sorts of small animals, from insects to mammals and birds.
- Hawks are normally solitary, but a group circling in air currents is called a *kettle*.
- Hawks like to nest high above the ground.

PLOVER

- Plovers are shorebirds that can also be found on mudflats and on the tundra.
- Their diet includes vegetation, seeds, insects, and small animals.
- Baby plovers leave the nest 3 hours after they hatch, but return for several days before leaving for good.
- Plovers nest in a shell-lined indention on the ground.

EAGLE

- Two types of eagles are found in North America: Bald and Golden.
- Eagles are carnivores that eat both live prey and carrion.
- The Bald Eagle was adopted as the U.S. symbol in 1782.
- Eagles make very large nests. One Golden Eagle nest was 20 feet tall and 8.5 feet wide. Bald Eagle nests are usually closer to 3 feet tall and 5 or 6 feet around.

COWBIRD

- Brown-Headed Cowbirds are common across the U.S., especially on farmland.
- Along with a diet of insects, seeds, and grains, females eat snail shells and other birds' eggshells.
- They need the calcium from these shells to form strong eggshells of their own because they can lay up to 3 dozen eggs in a season.
- Cowbirds don't make nests. Instead, they lay their eggs in other birds' nests.

KILLDEER

- This shorebird can be seen all over North America, and not just on the shore.
- They eat mostly invertebrates.
- To lure predators away from their eggs, killdeer act like easy prey by faking a broken wing.
- To keep animals like cows from stepping on their nests, killdeer puff up and charge.

For Janet Grenzke and Don Kroodzma
and all their grandbaby birds.

For Greg Budney, who brings birdsong
to everyone at The Cornell Lab of Ornithology and
brought it inside our home when we needed it.

And mostly, for our very own birdman,
David Stemple—beloved husband and father.

—*JY & HEYS*

To my favorite little nestlings, Azalea, Milo,
and Lulu —*MS*

Text copyright © 2015 by Jane Yolen and Heidi E.Y. Stemple
Illustrations copyright © 2015 by Melissa Sweet
All rights reserved
For information about permission to reproduce selections from
this book, contact permissions@highlights.com.

Boyds Mills Press
An Imprint of Highlights
815 Church Street
Honesdale, Pennsylvania 18431

Printed in China
ISBN: 978-1-59078-923-0
Library of Congress Control Number: 2014943965

First edition
Design by Barbara Grzeslo
Production by Margaret Mosomillo
The text of this book is set in Bembo.
The illustrations are done in watercolor,
gouache, and mixed media.

10 9 8 7 6 5 4 3 2 1